ANGEL CHILD

ANGEL CHILD

by Val Teal

Pictures by Pelagie Doane

RAND McNALLY & COMPANY

New York · CHICAGO · San Francisco

One day some angels were playing on a cloud. There were big angels and little angels and one who was only a baby.

The big angels kept saying, "Now stay right here on this big white cloud. Those small dark ones have rain in them, and if you get on them you'll get your wings wet."

The baby angel thought he'd like to see the rain, so he wandered to the edge of the big white cloud and peeped over. He leaned over too far!

He would have fallen if it hadn't been for his wings. But his wings let him fly quietly to one of the small dark clouds.

He landed on it gently and didn't get his wings wet at all. So he stayed there and sailed along on the little black cloud.

It was fun to be alone. The cloud flew down low and the baby angel could see the sights on the earth below.

He had a lovely time sailing along over town
and country with the cool, soft cloud to rest on
as he flew.

But then the cloud flew lower and suddenly, before he knew it, the baby angel dropped — *smack!* — into a tree. The cloud burst, and the rain went everywhere, especially on the baby angel's wings.

He couldn't fly one bit with heavy, wet wings, and besides, his beautiful blue robe was caught on a branch.

He started to cry.

Peter and Patty were playing beneath the tree. When they felt the rain and heard the crying, they looked up.

They were a little surprised to see an angel
caught in their tree. They felt sorry for him.
"We'll get you down," they called.

So they ran to Peter's mother, who was lying down with a cold cloth on her head. They said, "There's a baby angel caught in our tree. Come and get him down."

But Peter's mother said, "Run along, please, and don't bother me. I have *such* a headache."

Then they went to Patty's mother, but she was having a party and wouldn't listen.

So they got a ladder. And Patty held it while
Peter went up, and the baby angel stopped cry-
ing and put his arms around Peter's neck, and
Peter pulled him off and backed down with him.

The baby angel's robe was all torn, and Peter and Patty wondered what they should do about it. It didn't look nice at all, the way the angel showed through.

Patty said, "Have you got a safety pin, Peter?"

Peter had one where the button was gone from the side of his suit. So he unpinned it.

But one wasn't enough, so Patty took one off her garter.

Peter pinned up the baby angel's torn robe
while Patty comforted him. She said, "Don't
cry, Angel Child."

So he didn't cry.

"What shall we do with him?" Peter said.

And Patty said, "We'll give him to your mother. She wants a baby. She said she might get one in the fall."

But Peter said, "I don't know if she'll like one with wings."

"We'll put one of your sleepers on him,"
Patty said, "and that will cover up his wings."

Then Peter said, "But what about baths?"

And Patty said, "Oh, your mother will be
so fond of him by bath time that she won't mind,
even if she does notice the wings."

They took Angel Child in through the
kitchen and up the back stairs. Magnolia, the
cook, was so surprised that she spilled the
pudding she was making.

Peter and Patty put a sleeper on Angel Child and got the wings inside, but they made a hump.

They put him in the little bed Peter used to have. His mother had it ready for the baby she might get in the fall.

But Angel Child didn't want to lie in a bed with his wings buttoned in. He cried and cried.

Peter and Patty were afraid he might wake Peter's mother, so they took him out of bed.

They decided they would have to get him good and sleepy first.

They knew that baths made people sleepy, so they put Angel Child into the bathtub. They ran warm water on him and washed him good all over, his wings, too.

Peter's mother heard them. She called down to Magnolia, "What *are* those children doing?"

And Magnolia said, "They're doing no harm, the darlings. Those blessed children are getting better every day."

When Peter and Patty got Angel Child all
dry except his wings, which were hard to dry,
they put his robe back on him.

They went outdoors and played hide-and-go-seek, but Angel Child didn't know how to play. When they couldn't find him, he'd come out and help them look. So that was no fun.

Then they let him ride in Peter's automobile, but his wings were in the way.

So Patty got her tricycle, but his feet didn't reach the pedals.

Then they put him in the swing. They told him to hold on tight and they both pushed. Angel Child liked that. He cooed and gurgled, and when it was Patty's turn he didn't want to get out.

So they swung him some more, because he was little. They swung him and swung him. And all the time Angel Child's wings kept getting drier and drier.

Pretty soon he unfolded them, and then
how high he did swing! He fluttered his wings
and went way up.

He folded them and went way back. And then he fluttered them and went way up, even higher.

And pretty soon he went so high that he went right over the top of the swing.

The rope twisted around the pole and broke!
But Angel Child didn't fall. He kept right
on going, because his wings were all dry.

And the last Peter and Patty saw of him, he was flying straight up, still holding on to the seat of the swing.

Peter's father thought some big boys must have broken the swing.

And Patty's mother said, "That child has lost another garter."

Peter and Patty felt very sad because Angel Child was gone.

In the fall, sure enough, Peter's mother did get a baby, just as she had said she might.

Peter and Patty went upstairs to see it. A nurse brought it out into the hall, because Peter's mother was in bed, not feeling very well.

"It's Angel Child!" Peter and Patty both said at once when they saw him.

"Let's see the back of him," Patty said.

But his back was just plain, without wings.

"Anyway, he *is* Angel Child, isn't he?" Patty asked.

And the nurse said, "Of course he's an angel child."

So they knew he was.